# DOWN BY JIM LONG'S STAGE

# DOWN BY
# JIM LONG'S
# STAGE

Rhymes
for children and young fish

By Al Pittman
New illustrations by Pam Hall

Breakwater
100 Water Street
P.O. Box 2188
St. John's, NF
A1C 6E6

### Canadian Cataloguing in Publication Data

Pittman, Al, 1940-
 Down by Jim Long's stage: rhymes for children and young fish
  ISBN 1-55081-163-0
 I. Fishes--Juvenile poetry. 2. Children's poetry, Canadian
  (English) 3. Humourous poetry, Canadian (English) I. Hall, Pam
  PS8531.I86D62001     C811'.54     C2001-9OO351-X
  PZ8.3.P558684Do2001

The Canada Council | Le Conseil des Arts
for the Arts | du Canada

We acknowledge the financial support of The Canada Council for the Arts
for our publishing activities.

Reprinted in 2011

 We acknowledge the financial support of the Government of Canada through the Book Publishing Industry Development Program (BPIDP) for our publishing activities.

Printed in Canada.

This book is for Kyran
who read it first and Emily,
who listened smiling.


These pictures are for Jordan—
who missed them the first time,
and inspired them the second—
Follow the path.

Rodney Cod
oh so odd
all dressed up
in seaweed sod.

Off he went
to the bottom of the sea
saying,
"Wouldn't you like to be
just like me?"

In rows of fives
and rows of tens,
there they sit
those cocks and hens.

If you can't see them,
do not pout.
You'll see them
when the tide goes out.

Ella Eel
so long
and slinky
met a squid
whose name
was Inky.

"Oh my!"
said Ella
slinking by
when Inky
inked her
in the eye.

Rosie Rosefish
went to bed,
a dream of roses
in her head.

She dreamt how
lovely it would be
to plant a garden
in the sea.

Donald Dogfish
chased a catfish
round and round the sea.

He chased her
'til he chased her
up a seaweed
apple tree.

A lobster named Larry
so wanted to marry
Lila the lobster next door.

That when he proposed
and she turned up her nose,
he wept all over the floor.

Lucy Lumpfish
wobbled back and forth,
wobbled west and
wobbled north.

She wondered
as she wobbled
how wobbly
she would be
if she wobbled
all the way
to a wedding
in La Scie.

LaScie

Sid Squid
went and hid
behind a sunken dory.

His wife came out
and gave him a clout.
And Sid said he was sorry.

SPAIN

Zoro was a swordfish,
a roving hero bold.
He roved along the
Spanish Main
and captured pirate gold.

His neighbours,
they all laughed at him,
they thought him
rather silly.
Because, in fact,
he was a smelt
and lived in Piccadilly.

PICCADILLY

Cabot Codfish
on a snooze
dreamt Jim Long
ate fish and brewis.

And in his dream
for goodness sake
Jim Long got
a stomach ache.

Young Clem Clam
thought as he swam
as clumsy
as ever he could.

How he did wish
he was shaped
like a fish
and could swim
wherever he would.

Walter was a wolf fish.
A ferocious fish was he.
He growled and growled
and growled and growled
his way around the sea.

The other fish ignored him
which made him awful sore.
So Walter growled
and growled,
and growled
'til he could growl
no more.

Russell Mussell
opened his door
and looked out
on the ocean floor.

He got such
an awful fright
to see two lobsters
in a fight,
that Russell Mussell
slammed his door
and never looked out
on the floor no more.

Roger was a razor fish
as sharp as he could be.
He said to Calvin Catfish,
"I'll shave you for a fee."

"No thanks,"
said Calvin Catfish,
"I like me like I be."
And with his whiskers
on his face
he headed out to sea.

ST. PIERRE

René was a wrinkle.
He came from St. Pierre.

PUSHTHROUGH

He settled down
in Pushthrough
with his wrinkle
lady fair.

A sculpin named Sam
thought as he swam
how wonderful ugly
was he.

He said with a grin,
"I'm as ugly as sin."

"I'm the ugliest fish
in the sea."

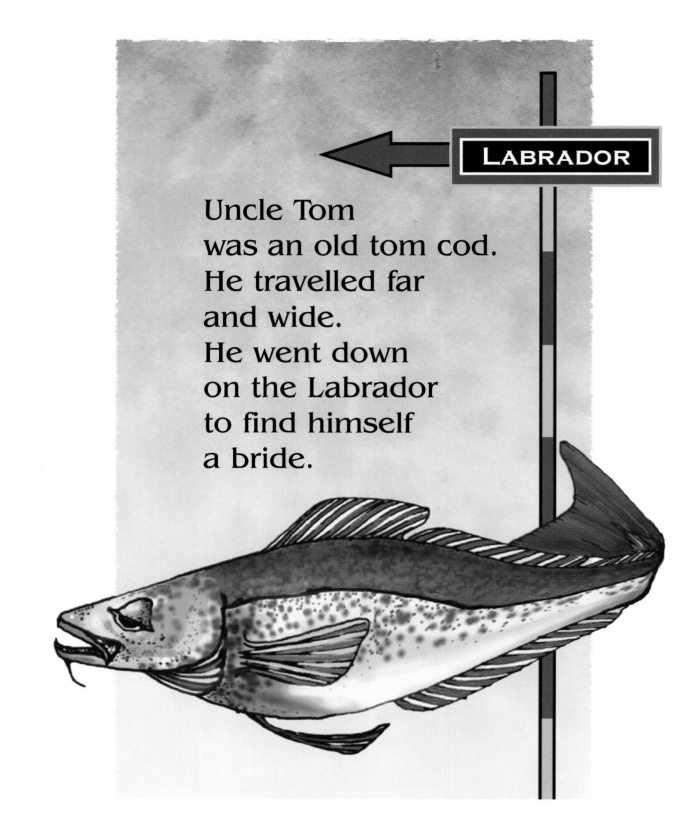

LABRADOR

Uncle Tom
was an old tom cod.
He travelled far
and wide.
He went down
on the Labrador
to find himself
a bride.

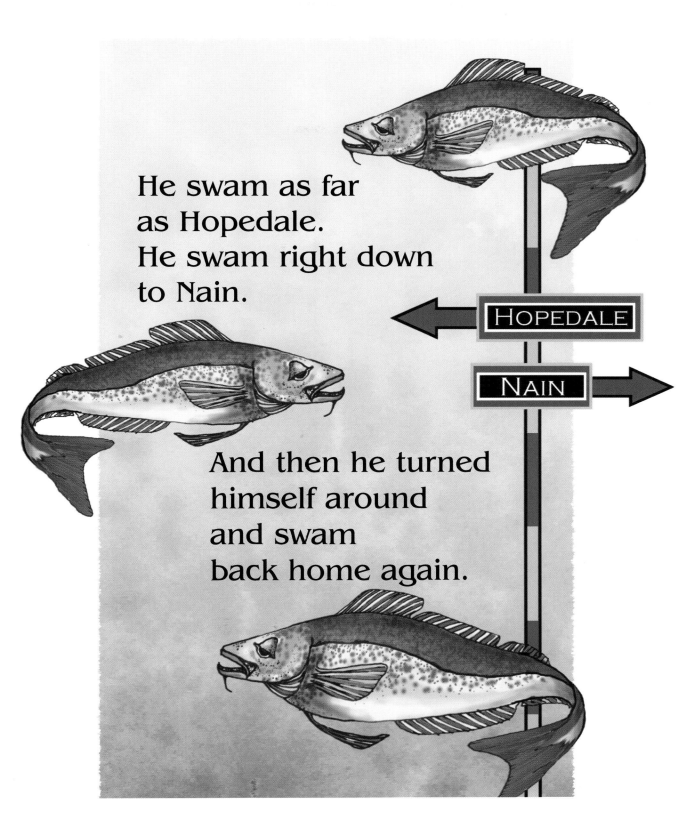

He swam as far
as Hopedale.
He swam right down
to Nain.

HOPEDALE

NAIN

And then he turned
himself around
and swam
back home again.

A flatfish named Fred,
when he rolled out of bed,
went soundly asleep
on the floor.

When called by his mother,
his sister and brother,
he answered them all
with a snore.

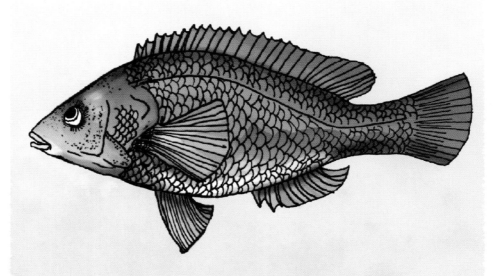

Connie Conner's cousin Cora
had a friend
whose name was Laura.

Said Cora to Laura,
"I'll see ya tomorra
down by Jim Long's stage."